PAYTON'S RUN

A SECURITY DIRECTORATE SHORT STORY

ALEXANDRIA BLAELOCK

Also by Alexandria Blaelock

SHORT STORY COLLECTIONS
The Histories of Hayward Hall
Lovelorn, Lovestruck and Love at First Sight
Common or Garden Variety Heroes
Case Files of the Wilkinson Detective Agency
Unavoidable Fates
Christmas Travesties
Five Faces of Felicia Clarke
Little Place Called Home

FICTION
That Love Nonsense
Taipan vs Brown
The Ghost and Ms Cox
Friends Like That

MS BLAELOCK'S BOOKS
Stress Free Dinner Parties
Signature Wardrobe Planning
Holistic Personal Finance
Minimally Viable Housekeeping
Planning a Life Worth Living

A SELECTION OF AVAILABLE SHORT STORIES
Alma's Grace
Fate in Your Hands
Lady of the Looking Glass
Morning Star, Evening Star, Superstar
Secret Singer
Shining Star
Ship in a Bottle
Simone Says Hands in the Air
The Day the Schedule Broke

For permission requests, please contact
enquiries@bluemerebooks.com.

Ordering Information:
Discounts are available on quantity purchases. For details, contact orders@bluemerebooks.com.

Payton's Run/Alexandria Blaelock
paperback ISBN: 978-1-925749-24-3
digital ISBN: 978-1-925749-25-0

Book Layout © BookDesignTemplates.com
Cover Art © Tithi Luadthong/Depositphotos

PAYTON'S RUN

A SECURITY DIRECTORATE
SHORT STORY

ALEXANDRIA BLAELOCK

BlueMere Books
MELBOURNE, AUSTRALIA

PAYTON'S RUN

Payton finished retying her shoelaces, and not for the first time queried the necessity of heeled walking shoes.

There was no doubt they were strikingly elegant. Perhaps a little intimidating, in combination with the navy blue tactical uniform of kick pleated pencil skirt suit.

But not necessarily practical.

Which was, of course, why you wore the uniform for all physical training classes.

After graduation, you were always on duty, and never knew when you'd need to chase someone down.

If you wanted to maintain your authority in all circumstances, you had to adapt to the uniform's limitations so completely you could safely react in an instant.

No one respects or fears a woman in a torn skirt, and you needed people to look up to you, not down on you.

Her fitted jacket absorbed the warmth of the sun, releasing the odour of dry cleaning chemicals.

Which was, of course, the other downside of physical training - the cost of keeping your uniform clean and fresh was astronomical.

Some students cheated and saved one jacket just for the physical classes, but she was a little too fastidious for that.

Not to mention you never knew when the Generals would make a surprise inspection and they frowned on that kind of sloppiness.

The uniform was a symbol of the Protection Squad's ultimate power, to be treated with reverence and cared for properly.

Lest you find yourself on the wrong side of it.

Improper dress was one of many ways to pick up demerit points. If you accrued enough of them, you'd be expelled from the University of Civilisation.

And despite having passed the Genomics Bureau post-natal testing, and surviving the State Academy of Cultural Regulation, expulsion was the end of your high-level career.

The Directorate didn't permit rogues with the kind of genetic abilities known colloquially as "superpowers" to go free.

If you were "lucky", you'd be forcibly lobotomised, and get a place in the lower ranks of the Protection Squadron. Your life would be short, but you'd be taken care of.

If you weren't lucky, you'd be shunted into the euthanasia programme, and that would be the end of you.

Payton closed her eyes and turned to face the sun. Its warmth offset the cool breeze, and it was a pleasant day.

The kind of day normals would go for country walks, picnics or punting on the river.

No such luxury for her.

Her physical final was fast approaching, and a lot was riding on it.

There were no second chances; if she failed the physical, she'd fail her course, and wouldn't graduate.

Which would be the end of her career.

Payton marched onto the freshly mown sports ground. She smoothed her skirt across her hips, checked to make sure all her jacket buttons were secured, and adjusted the placement of her hat.

Then she checked her practice firearm was loaded with pellets, and the safety was on.

She couldn't just scrape a pass in the physical exam either. The physical prowess and endurance she demonstrated had a direct bearing on her first and future placements.

Which made the stakes higher, because physical training was not one of her better subjects.

Despite the weight training, her slight physique made it difficult to cope with some of the physical obstructions.

But it was useful for escape scenarios and encouraged other people to underestimate her abilities.

Plus, she'd learned to leverage her body weight and strength for advantage in hand-to-hand combat.

She made it look easy, but it was gruelling work.

Having completed a lap of the oval, she stood on the grass to complete her warm-up.

Standing, with her feet shoulder-width apart, she rotated her head across her shoulders, grunting a little as her stiff neck protested from the pain of crouching over her desk for the last few weeks cramming for her academic finals.

She rotated her shoulder joints backwards and forwards, followed by her elbows, wrists, hips, knees and ankles.

Then some dynamic stretches, focusing on stretching her arms and wrists to their maximum, hamstrings, bending from the hips to touch her toes, and finishing with some lunges.

As she stretched, she reflected that while her uniform was restrictive; it offered the practical benefits of compression and leverage.

Maybe that was the key lesson of the physical component, learning how to make the best use of the limited materials that were available to you.

And why no additional protective gear was permitted during the exercises; it was unlikely they'd be available to you during the usual course of your duties.

With her warm-up complete, she took a deep breath and used her University identification card to swipe into the training village.

She walked down the main street, carefully surveying the terrain.

It had once been a vibrant local community, but during the Bread Riots decades earlier, the surviving villagers had been driven out and not permitted to return.

Sounds harsh, but alive and hungry is better than dead and dead.

The village had been left to deteriorate until the University acquired the land for Urban Warfare training.

Automated training exercises included both offensive and defensive manoeuvres, and she'd booked both for her hour-long session.

While she'd been through the village several times, she couldn't predict what she'd find. To ensure a semi-realistic scenario, they programmed the physical and holographic hazards to activate randomly in response to your actions.

There would be targets that flipped and ran, there might be weather events, collapsing buildings, or explosions.

And as a final year student, the safety would be off, so she'd be facing live ammunition with the real possibility of injury or even death.

Payton was comfortable with the risk, she wouldn't be training otherwise.

And she enjoyed the combination of intellectual analysis and gut instinct, hoping her first job would involve a placement where she could use these skills.

As she strolled, seemingly unconcerned, down the footpath close to the buildings, her navy uniform melted into the shadows.

She looked in the windows, assessing the reflected environment for unusual signs of movement, listened for sounds, and sniffed for odours that might indicate an attack.

As a Protection Squad Officer, there was always a fine line between her presence as a visible deterrent/target and the need for covert operations.

Something flashed to her left, and she ducked to reduce her target size.

She heard footsteps running down the street, but there was no telltale aroma of gunfire.

Whoever was running hadn't fired a shot. Was it a lure drawing her into a trap, or someone fleeing from the sight of her uniform?

She quickly scanned the street, noting it was quiet and clear.

The overpass further down could obstruct her line of sight, offering the potential of an ambush.

She looked up at the building she was sheltering below and thought the third-story window offered a good sniper position with the correct trajectory for a kill shot near the overpass.

Payton didn't think she'd survive the overpass and chose to enter the building to clear the possible sniper.

She withdrew her weapon and eased slowly through the door, giving her eyes time to adjust to the gloom inside.

Clearing the room would be quicker and easier with an assault team, but she had no choice but to proceed alone.

She'd have to weigh each decision carefully.

The foyer appeared clear, so she turned left towards the staircase.

It was on the external wall, with light streaming through the tall, slightly opaque safety glass windows.

She glanced up to see a solid roof and understood an attack could only come from the front and rear.

Senses straining, trying to avoid silhouetting herself against the windows, she rapidly climbed from the ground to the third floor and approached the sniper's nest.

Hearing a faint sigh, she spun around, but the target was a secretary with a stack of files. She pointed it back towards the office it came from, and it slid obediently away.

The slight movement was enough to warn the sniper, and a volley of shots broke out.

Payton dropped to the floor, rolled onto her stomach, and crawled closer to the door.

At that moment, it flew open, and a holographic sniper ran from the room. She rolled and shot up at it until it fell.

She checked it was dead before entering the room to find it empty.

That was the first target secured.

Before leaving, she stood beside the window, looking down the street for other potential hazards, and found none.

It seemed safe to proceed.

But she was running out of time.

As she retreated to the stairs, she decided to go up rather than down.

At the top, she found a small door out onto the roof, and opening it a crack, looked down over the grey rooftops and terracotta chimney pots.

There were no readily identifiable hazards. It was a beautiful day, and the village looked charming from above, so she decided to finish with a race across the rooftops.

Avoiding the church she made directly for the exit, so the rest of her session passed relatively uneventfully.

She ran lightly across the rooftops, somersaulting across gaps between buildings, and sliding down the ridgelines.

Now and again, there was a potshot from the street below or a passing thug target to shoot down.

Occasionally, just for fun, she'd flip and run up or down a wall.

After exiting the village, she stopped outside the Debriefing Centre to do some static stretches and shake out her limbs to cool down her tired muscles.

Then went inside, washed her face and tidied her hair before reviewing her performance.

"Nice job Cadet," said the officer in attendance, exchanging her practice firearm for a restorative drink and her assessment print out.

"If you have any questions, come back to me."

She nodded, took the paper and drink to a table where she sat and read the report.

She'd taken a few minutes more than an hour to complete the course.

Not too bad, though if you didn't exit on time, you risked being caught up in and graded for someone else's exercise.

She'd "killed" all the essential targets along her route, "spared" the right number of civilians, used a reasonable amount of ammunition to achieve her objectives.

All in all, not too bad, though it was hard to know how useful that exercise would be for her final.

It didn't feel like she'd done much, but her body and brain were tired, and she wanted a hot shower.

There'd be enough time for a recovery nap before dinner.

She adjusted the set of her uniform and nodded at the officer as she left the building.

It was a long walk, uphill, around the village back to the dorm, so there was plenty of time to consider the physical final.

All she knew was that now her final written and oral exams were over, the physical would take place during the next two weeks.

They tailored the scenario to your individual strengths and weaknesses. The Directorate's goal was to expose any impediments to the potential careers plotted out for you.

It might be a hostage rescue, taking down a criminal kingpin, or stealing an item of significance.

It would be a live scenario through an inhabited area, relying only on her physical abilities, no superpowers permitted.

During the event, she'd endure various armed and unarmed assaults, during which they expected her to achieve her objective while harming no citizens.

If she were injured or killed, she'd fail.

If she didn't capture her target, she'd fail.

If she harmed innocent citizens, she'd fail.

She wouldn't know who, if anyone, she could trust or rely on.

The prospect was terrifying, but theoretically, she had all the skills she needed.

And while her recent exercise had been uneventful, perhaps that indicated good strategic thinking.

No matter what else happened, it was best to minimise the risks to herself and others as much as possible and come out at the end unharmed.

Even if it felt like cheating.

She was caught off guard when someone grabbed her from behind, pinning her arms to her body, and roughly pulling a bag over her head.

Her mind went blank, and she froze for an instant, but it was long enough to be bundled into a vehicle, and hear the back doors slam.

She couldn't tell how many men were in the van, or what language they were speaking, but her struggled attempt to break free, and escape, was met with a solid punch to the guts that took the wind out of her.

Someone banged on the wall.

The engine roared, and tyres squealed as the vehicle started moving.

They took advantage of her weakness to tape up her wrists, but while she couldn't breathe or fight, her brain had kicked in.

She let her hands fall open as she crossed her wrists to maximise their size and leave some room to break the tape.

As her captors moved to tape her ankles, she tensed them to increase their size and held them a little apart so that the tape would also be a little loser.

As she caught her gasping breath, she started sobbing, and they laughed derisively.

As if in response, she rolled to face the wall of the van and curled protectively around her belly.

They seemed to think her defeated, and aside from a half-hearted kick, let her be.

They huddled somewhere nearby discussing something, but the tones of their voices didn't suggest she was in immediate danger.

The most likely scenario was being taken to a secondary location for interrogation or ransom.

Or maybe both.

Whatever their plans, she needed to set herself free before they reached it.

As she started taking stock of her situation, one man lit a cigarette, while another made a joke and they all laughed.

So, she was in a closed compartment with three men. The driver was not in it with them, and would need to be dealt with separately.

The door was at her feet, and it used a latch mechanism.

She was fully dressed, lying on some sort of rough fabric, hands and feet bound.

Her hands were bound in front of her.

If she was relatively still, they might interpret her movements as swaying with the vehicle rather than attempting to free herself.

The hood was still on her head, but the weave was loose and she could discern shapes, and probably movement around her.

The smooth ride and sound of the tyres suggested an asphalt road, and the frequent pauses, acceleration and deceleration suggested they were driving on city streets.

The best option was to free herself before the vehicle left the confines of the City.

That meant freeing her feet and getting out of the vehicle were the critical tasks.

Once she was running, she could free her hands, lose herself in the crowds of citizens, and make her way back to campus.

And the quickest way to do that was to leave her hat behind and unpin her hair.

Demerit points be dammed!

While she didn't have a firearm, she had a razor blade concealed in the heel of her left shoe.

And at this moment, trussed up in this van, she was grateful the heels offered her more than a slim calf and sexy stance.

Though it wouldn't be easy to get at it. Should have practised more in her spare time.

Another joke suggested her guards were amateurs and wouldn't be carefully watching her.

She risked bending further to reach her feet while nodding her head a little in time to the vehicle's movements to loosen her hat and partially roll up the hood.

So far, so good.

She got the blade free and cut the tape, but didn't kick it off immediately. At a glance, it would look secure, yet be easy to kick off when the time came.

In the meantime, she carefully tucked the blade between the fingers of her right hand in case she needed it as a weapon.

Still gently moving her head, she dislodged her hat. If she sat up rapidly, the weight of it should pull the hood off so she could see what she was doing.

Her captors were still talking, and she hadn't heard anything to suggest there were weapons, so it might be possible to get a second or two ahead of them.

Now that she'd worked through a scenario, she was ready to put it into action.

The vehicle slowed, and she tensed her muscles.

When the vehicle stopped, she sat up rapidly, losing the hood.

Then she leaned forward, dug one heel into the floor and leveraged herself into a crouch from which she could open the door with her bound hands.

As she half fell, half stepped out of the vehicle, she quickly assessed the new environment.

There were shops nearby, with plenty of civilians coming and going.

There was a large department store a little further down the street, so she ran towards it.

As she ran, she lifted her hands and abruptly pulled them down towards her abdomen, using her body as a wedge to tear the tape open.

She heard the men shouting behind her, and a few shots fired, but made it to the store unharmed.

She bolted inside, tearing the pins out of her hair, and fluffing it up, so her waist-length locks hung freely down her back.

Aware that they'd be looking for someone in uniform running, she headed towards the centre of the ground floor, unbuttoning her jacket and blouse.

As she passed a display table, she grabbed a bright floral scarf and wound it around her neck.

Moving past another, she added some jangly bracelets for her wrists.

She took a large flower pin from a third and pinned it in her hair as she picked up a brightly coloured handbag from a fourth.

Then layered in a generous spray of an intense oriental fragrance on her way to the makeup counter.

She snatched up cosmetics here and there and applied them thickly.

As she turned to inspect herself in the mirror, a man in rough tradesman clothing and a baseball cap rudely pushed her out of the way.

Was he one of her kidnappers?

She continued sauntering through the ground floor towards an exit on the other side.

The security guard looked like he was going to arrest her, so she flashed her Protection Squad identification, and he stood down.

She debated for a moment whether to inform him of the kidnappers, but decided that would waste valuable escape time.

She'd be better able to access her memories under interrogation back at the University, anyway.

She nodded at the guard and left the store, just in time to jump on a bus heading towards the University.

Taking a seat, she closed her eyes for a moment in relief at having escaped.

Seemingly safe, but still on edge.

She thought she heard shouting, but didn't risk turning to see what the commotion was about.

It was several stops before she could relax enough to slump in the seat and take some long, slow breaths to dissipate the tension in her neck and shoulders.

Arriving back at the University, she wasn't exactly sure whether to report the kidnapping immediately or clean up first.

But the campus police decided for her.

"Ma'am, you're out of uniform. Please follow us to the Disciplinary Unit."

Payton nodded assent and fell in.

Now that she was back on campus, she was more than happy to let someone else take the lead.

In any case, she was too tired to argue, and at least this way she'd get something to drink and her interrogation would be over sooner.

The officer escorted her through the door and gestured towards an interview room.

"Please wait here, Ma'am," he said, opening the door and closing it behind her.

She set the stolen bag on the table, then removed the rest of her disguise piece by piece, folding it carefully and laying it out in a row.

She was attempting to secure her hair when the door opened and her academic supervisor entered.

She dropped her hair and saluted smartly.

"Congratulations Lieutenant, you've passed both your academic and physical examinations and are approved for graduation."

She broke into a wide grin as he pulled a small box from his pocket and continued, "I'm authorised to pin your official insignia to your uniform."

He unbuttoned and removed the unadorned shoulder boards from her jacket, and replaced them with her new one pip boards, before taking a step back and saluting.

She returned his salute.

"Your orders will arrive in the next few days, so in the meantime, relax and celebrate before the hard work begins."

THE END

ABOUT THE AUTHOR

Alexandria Blaelock writes stories, some of them for *Ellery Queen's Mystery Magazine* and *Pulphouse Fiction Magazine*.

She's also written five selfhelp books applying business techniques to personal matters like getting dressed, cleaning house, and feeding your friends.

She lives in a forest because she enjoys birdsong, and the smell of gum leaves. When not telecommuting to parallel universes from her Melbourne based imagination, she watches K-dramas, talks to animals, and drinks Campari. At the same time.

Discover more at www.alexandriablaelock.com.

IF YOU ENJOYED THIS STORY...

try the other Security Directorate stories

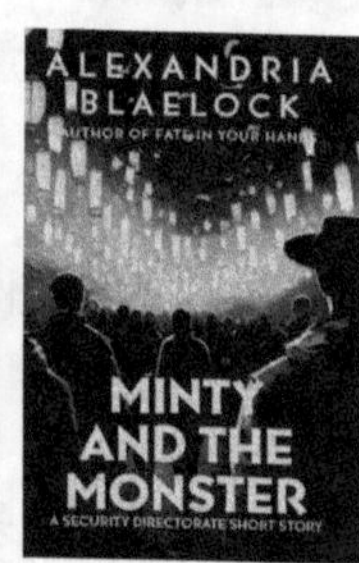

... or the collections

Why not try The Ghost and Ms Cox

Life interrupted

To say the letter was a surprise was an understatement. It arrived addressed to Miss Finlay Cox, which made the contents even more extraordinary.

Orphan Finn Cox inherits a cottage. Thinks it holds the key to her origins. Of course she takes a look. Who wouldn't?

But when she gets there, she gets more than she bargained for.

Is it friend, family or foe?